CARMINE THE CROW

To
Sam Howard Pepper
and
the memory of
Augie, Rosie, and Cybele

CARMINE THE CROW

HEIDI HOLDER

Farrar, Straus and Giroux
New York

Carmine the Crow was a very old crow and he lived in a very old tree. He loved to collect shiny objects and had masses of glittery things in his attic: thimbles, beads, keys, anything with a glint or a glimmer. He was especially fond of his tinfoil collection.

One day, while he was searching for things in the forest, he met Millie the Mink.

"What are you doing, Millie?"

"I am thinking about the wonderful party at Possum's house tomorrow. It's his birthday and all the animals are going. You are going, too, aren't you, Carmine?"

Carmine sighed. "No, my friend, I am not. I would be out of place at such a splendid party. My feathers are all tattered. I have no money to buy Possum a gift, and furthermore, I have no lady friend to go with me."

"Poor Carmine," said Millie. "Won't you come with Willie the Weasel and me?"

"No, thank you, my dear Millie. I just cannot go," said Carmine, and he flapped off through the forest.

He flew to a lonesome meadow and tramped through the grass looking for shiny bits and pieces of lost and forgotten things. He searched the whole day without finding even a button, and by evening he was very sad and tired.

Resting on a low stone, he hummed an old crow ballad to cheer himself up. Suddenly he heard a delicate voice calling desperately, "Help! Help!"

Carmine searched over the darkling meadow and then he gasped in wonder.

There, on the other side of a hill, was a beautiful swan, her wings glowing like moonlight.

"Help me!" she cried, and Carmine saw that her legs were tangled in a hunter's snare.

"I will help you. Do not fear!" called Carmine, and forgetting his weariness, he flew back to his nest.

He rummaged through his collection until he found an old pair of scissors.

"I knew these would come in handy someday," said Carmine as he hurried back to the swan and set her free.

"You have saved my life," said the swan, "and now I will repay your kindness."

The swan drew forth a small blue box and gave it to Carmine. He lifted the lid and was dazzled. For inside the box was a glittering, shimmering radiance.

The swan said, "This is stardust. It is very ancient. Sprinkle a pinch of it under your pillow at night and make a wish. In the morning, your wish will come true."

"Oh, heavenly bird, I thank you from the bottom of my heart," said Carmine.

Then the swan flew up into the sky, higher and higher, until she disappeared into the distant twilight.

Carmine's heart was beating. "My, my!" he thought. "This is surely the shiniest dust I have ever seen! Let me think. What shall I wish for, first? I think I will wish to be a handsome bird with glossy feathers. Then I will wish to be rich, and then I will wish for a wife."

And Carmine walked through the meadow, lost in happy thoughts.

As he walked along, he happened to meet a mouse who was weeping bitterly.

"What is the matter, little one?" asked Carmine.

The mouse cried, "Tomorrow is Possum's birthday party, but I cannot go. My tail is so short, all the other animals laugh and make fun of me."

"Weep no more, my tiny one," said Carmine, and he opened the box of stardust, saying, "Put some of this under your pillow and make a wish. In the morning, your wish will come true."

"Thank you. Thank you," squeaked the mouse, taking a big pinch of stardust. "I will wish for a long, beautiful tail." And she hurried away in delight.

Carmine walked on and soon he met a frog who was croaking miserably to himself.

"What is troubling you so?" asked Carmine.

The frog replied, "Tomorrow is Possum's birthday party, but I cannot go. I have no money to buy Possum a gift, and I cannot go without a gift. I have not even enough money to buy my children one small tin of fly biscuits."

"Here you are, my greenish friend," said Carmine, and he opened his box, saying, "This is stardust. Put a pinch under your pillow and make a wish. In the morning, your wish will come true."

"Thank you!" chortled the frog, and he took a big pinch. "I will wish for enough money to buy everybody presents!" And the frog leaped gleefully away.

Carmine traveled a little farther and came upon a lady rabbit crying forlornly into her hankie.

"What makes you so sad?" asked Carmine.

The rabbit sobbed, saying, "Tomorrow is Possum's birthday party, but I cannot go. Nobody loves me, so I have no one to go with, and I cannot go alone."

"Be sad no more, my long-eared lady," said Carmine, opening the box. Then Carmine stared in dismay at the stardust. There was only one pinch left. He started to close the box, but the lady rabbit asked, "What is that?"

Carmine looked at her tearstained face for a long time, shuffling his feathers this way and that. Then he sighed and said, "This, my dear, is stardust. Put it under your pillow and make a wish. In the morning, your wish will come true."

"How wonderful. Thank you!" cried the rabbit as she took the last pinch of stardust. "I will wish for someone to love and be loved by." And she hopped homeward, filled with happy dreams.

Carmine went home, too. Slowly he put the empty blue box high on a shelf and then he lay down to sleep. He slept, but he had no dreams.

The next day, Possum's party was a great success. Carmine hid himself in the branches of a tall tree overlooking Possum's garden, and watched all the animals laughing and dancing. He saw the mouse, the frog, and the rabbit, and it made him glad to see their wishes had indeed come true.

But, up in the high, shadowy leaves, Carmine felt a lonely ache in his heart. Occasionally he hummed an old crow ballad, but the ache just would not go away. He sat all day watching the animals, and when the sun went down and the stars and owls appeared, weariness overcame him and he flew home.

He made a cup of tea and drank it thoughtfully. The chill night air had made his wings stiff and he had a pain in his beak. He said to himself, "I am getting much too old and tired to look for shiny things. But I remember when I was young—I had such energy! I used to be able to fly to the big cities. I used to find so many glittery trinkets there and, oh, so much beautiful tinfoil!

"When I was young, my feathers were glossy and my beak was polished to a high, fine shine. And best of all, when I was young, I loved a sweet lady crow and she loved me."

Carmine sat with his eyes closed for many minutes. Then he rose and took down the empty box the swan had given him just yesterday. He set it on the kitchen table and lifted the lid.

He said softly, "I wish I could make a wish, but I cannot." And he looked at the box for a long, long time. In the silence of the night, the moon rose slowly and shone through Carmine's window. Its glow fell upon the box.

Suddenly . . . there! . . . In the corner of the box was a tiny, shiny glint! Carmine stared. One last grain of stardust gleamed in the moonlight.

Breathlessly, Carmine picked it up, and tottering over to his bed, he placed it under the pillow. He lay down and said, "I do not know if this will work, but oh, little speck of stardust, make my wish come true. Make me young again."

And in the morning, just as the sun was coming up,
Carmine's wish came true.